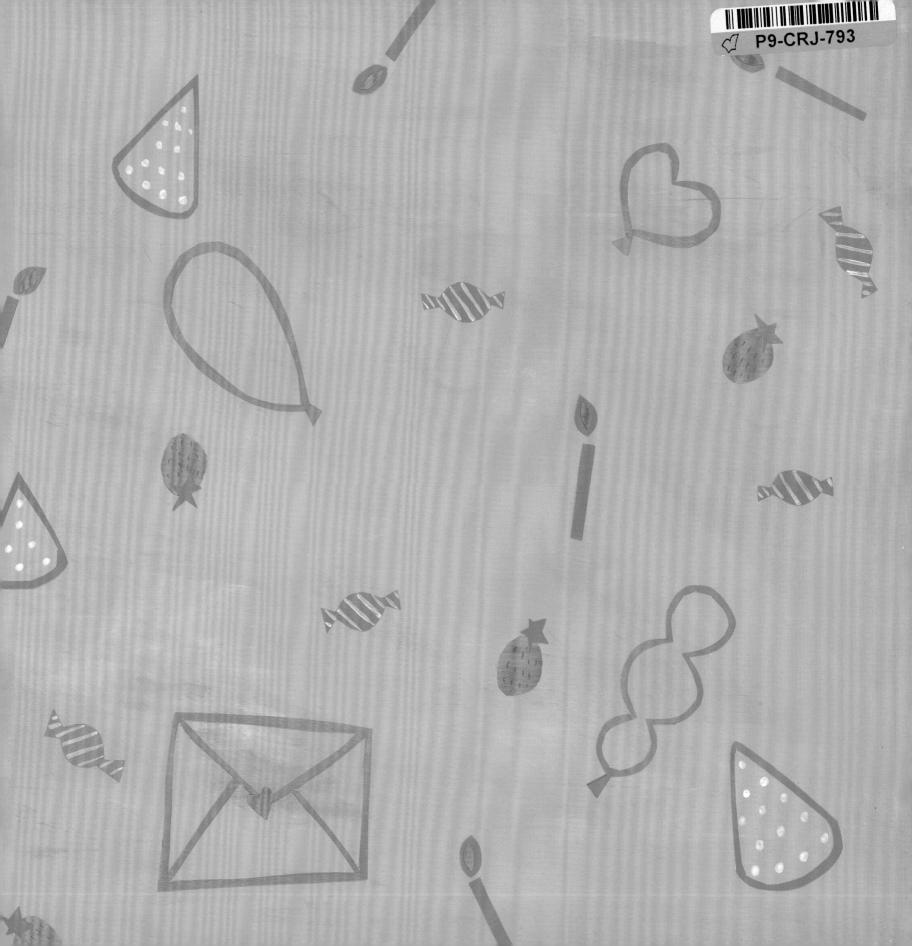

This picture book helps children learn about mathematical concepts through a colorful and entertaining story.

Math concepts explored may include:
• Understanding math concepts
• Numbers and operations
• Dealing with operations with mathematical signs ($\div$, $\times$, $+$, $-$): addition and subtraction

About the Author
Soon-jae Shin graduated from Ewha Womans University in Seoul, South Korea, with a degree in philosophy. She has worked for a publishing company for several years, and she has written many children's books.

About the Illustrator
Min-jung Kim graduated from Induk University with a degree in illustration. An active member of the illustrators' group A Scroll of Drawings, Min-jung has illustrated many children's books.

Tan Tan Math Story ***Ruffer's Birthday Party***

Original Korean edition © Yeowon Media Co., Ltd

This U.S edition published in 2015 by TANTAN PUBLISHING INC,
4005 W Olympic Blvd, Los Angeles, CA 90019-3258

U.S and Canada Edition © TANTAN PUBLISHING INC in 2015

ISBN: 978-1-939248-06-0

Printed in South Korea at Choil Munhwa Printing Co., 12 Seongsuiro 20 gil, Seongdong-gu, Seoul.

Ruffer's
Birthday Party

Written by Soon-jae Shin　　　　**Illustrated by Min-jung Kim**

✿TanTan Publishing

Ruffer's birthday is in just four more days. Ruffer is Nora's pet puppy and best friend. Nora is planning a birthday party for him—an awesome, unforgettable birthday party.

Nora is thinking about the party. "What should I do first?" she asks.

A birthday party? Ruffer is excited. He has never had a birthday party before.

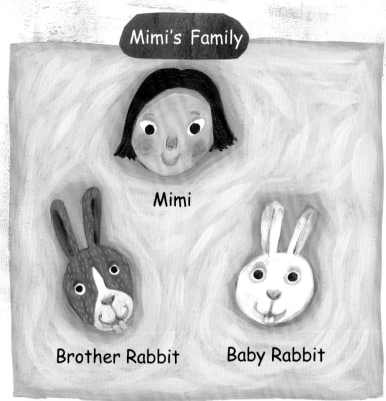

Mimi's Family

Mimi

Brother Rabbit

Baby Rabbit

Jamie's Family

Luna

Jamie

Felix

Isis

Snow

Zeus

Nancy's Family

Nancy

Mia

"Let's figure out how many invitations we need to make," says Nora.

To figure out the answer, Nora and Ruffer must add up all the friends they want to invite. That means they must add up everyone in all three families—Mimi's plus Jamie's plus Nancy's. Turning Nora's addition puzzle into a math problem means adding **3 plus 6 plus 2**.

The total is eleven guests, so we just need to make eleven invitations.

How did you figure that out so fast?

(Adding number)

(Adding number)

(Adding number)

(Added number)

$$3 + 6 + 2 = 11$$

This plus means "add together," or "put all the numbers together."

This plus means to add to the sum of 3 and 6, which equals 9. A sum is a total.

This means "equals."

Nora and Ruffer are eager to send out the invitations. They put them in the mailbox and head home. Along the way, they run into Nancy and Mia.

Mia, you have to come to our house in four days!

Why?

Because Ruffer is having a birthday party! Please come and celebrate with us.

Oh, really? That's so cool! We'll be there.

The next day, Mimi and the rabbits visit while Nora and Ruffer are making party hats.

The day after that, Jamie and the cats visit while Nora and Ruffer are cleaning the house.

The day after that, Mimi's rabbits and Jamie's cats visit.

At last, it is Ruffer's birthday! He has butterflies in his tummy—because he's so excited!

Nora is making a birthday cake. "This will be the most delicious puppy-cake in the world for my Ruffer!" she says.

10 cups of flour

Nora's Secret Recipe

4 tablespoons of sugar

?

10 eggs

2 bottles of milk   Fresh cream

Ta-da! It's my birthday cake recipe!

Humph. You left out the bones!

Eggs are an important ingredient in Nora's special cake! Ten eggs are needed to make the tastiest cake.

Nora must figure out how many more eggs she needs. She can find the answer by subtracting the number of eggs she has now from the total number of eggs she needs for her special cake.

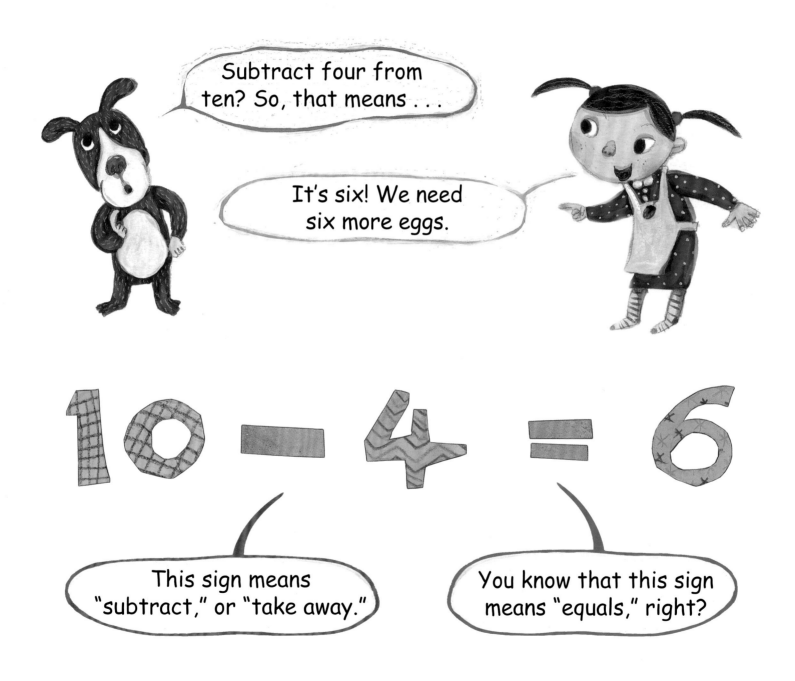

"We still need six eggs for the cake," Nora says. "We'll have to go to the store!"

Nora and Ruffer's friends will be arriving soon. The two of them must hurry to the store.

Ruffer, let's go to the supermarket to buy eggs.

Supermarket? You're going to buy me a juicy bone too, right? Today is my birthday, after all.

Crunch!

$$4 - 2 = 2$$

What was that *bad* sound?

Oh no! Ruffer accidentally stepped on the egg carton and broke too eggs!
How many more eggs does Nora need to buy now?

Oh, Ruffer!

Oh my, what was that doing down there?

Nora needs eight more
eggs. She decides to buy one
carton, which has ten eggs.

Nora and Ruffer rush to the supermarket. It's their lucky day! The supermarket is having its tenth-anniversary sale.

Nora is in a hurry to get the eggs! She needs to mix and then bake the cake before their friends arrive for the party.

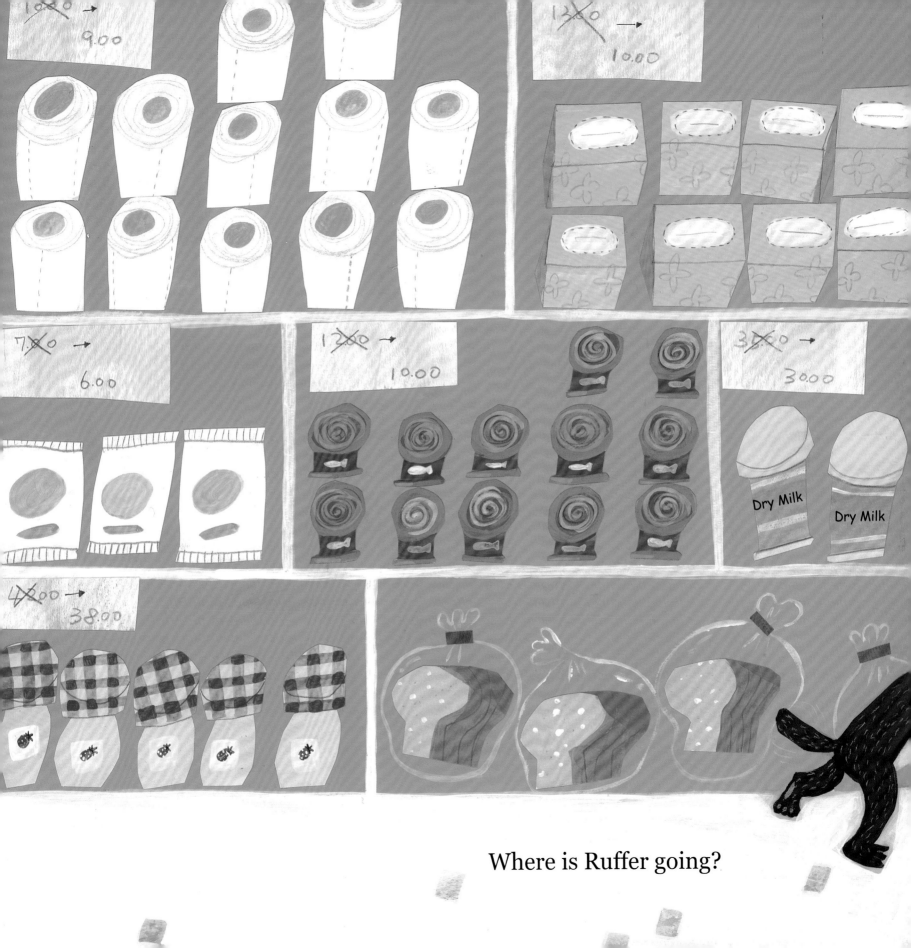

Where is Ruffer going?

Ruffer is hovering at the ice-cream counter—his favorite bone-chip ice cream is on sale!

A carton of bone-chip ice cream is usually five dollars, but Ruffer can save one dollar. Ruffer grabs one bone-chip ice cream, which is a good deal. How much will Ruffer need to pay for the bone-chip ice cream?

Ruffer moves along to the fruit section. He loves cream fruit cake more than anything in the world. He thinks about his birthday cake. "Yum—it would be fantastic to decorate it with fruit!" Ruffer says.

Mister, how much are the tangerines?

Tangerines $10
Today only: $8
↓
You save $2

Strawberries $10
Today only: $5
↓
You save $5

Bananas $10
Today only: $7
↓
You save $3

Tangerines are $10 per bag, but today's sale gives you $2 off.

Hmmm . . . Which fruit is the least expensive? Ruffer subtracts the sale amounts from the original prices.

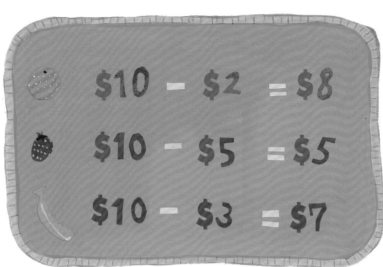

$10 − $2 = $8

$10 − $5 = $5

$10 − $3 = $7

Aha, so the strawberries are the cheapest! Mister, give me strawberries, please! It sure is good to know how to subtract.

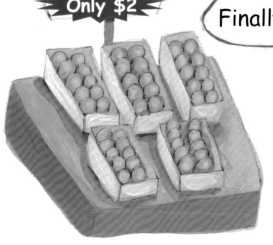

Eggs
$3 per carton
Today only:
You save $1
Only $2

Finally, here are the eggs!

Nora and Ruffer wonder how much money they've spent so far.
What is the total cost for all the items Nora and Ruffer bought?

Nora and Ruffer get the receipt from the cashier. The prices of all the items they bought are printed on it.

Receipt

I love sales!

Ice cream	$4
Strawberries	$5
Eggs	$2
Total	$11

The total is $11.

First, add the price of the ice cream and strawberries together, and then add the price of the eggs to that sum.

$4 + $5 = $9 + $2 = $11

Nora and Ruffer hurry home and bake the cake. Their friends arrive just as Nora finishes decorating it.

Ruffer's birthday party has begun at last! The party hats fit all the friends perfectly. Nora's cake is excellent. Her secret ingredient makes it extra special—chocolate cookie crumbs!

Ruffer's friends give him presents. He smiles from ear to ear when he sees the gifts. They are his very first birthday presents!

Ruffer gets busy organizing all the presents.
He sorts them into three categories.

Ruffer, stop looking at the presents and come play.

Hold on! Let me finish this first.

Ruffer's Birthday Present Chart

Bones		Stuffed animals		Balls	
🐰🐰	3	👧	1	🐵	2
👦	2	🐱	1	🐈‍⬛	+2
👧	1	🐱	+1		
🐱🐱	+3				
Total bones: 9		Total stuffed animals: 3		Total balls: 4	

After organizing his presents, Ruffer heads off to find his friends. "Hey, guys!" he says. "It's time for a fun game. First, we'll split into two teams."

What game will they play?

Game Rules

1. Six friends will make up each team.

2. Each team will get six rings.

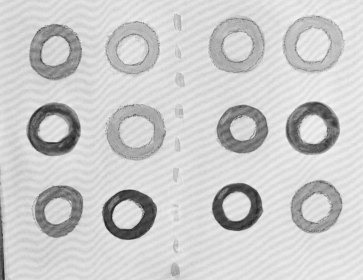

3. Each player will take turns throwing rings onto their team's pole.

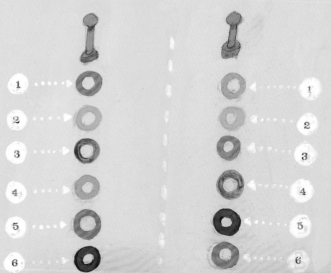

4. The team that has more rings on its pole wins.

Win | Lose

The game has started. The players on the Bone team are really good at tossing rings. The number of rings in their basket is getting smaller, but the number of rings on their pole is getting bigger! The poor players on the Food Bowl team are sad. Their rings keep falling to the ground.

Everyone had fun playing the game, but which team won? The Bone Team won, because the players got three more rings on their pole than the Food Bowl team did.

Ruffer's birthday party is over—but the friends will always remember the fun they had. Ruffer will remember his best-ever birthday most fondly of all!

Addition and Subtraction as Problem-Solving Methods

This story is about best friends Ruffer and Nora, who go to a supermarket to prepare for Ruffer's birthday party. The story can help children learn to use addition and subtraction in various real-life situations. It can also help them understand the practical use and value of mathematics.

Nora has a lot to do to get ready for Ruffer's party. The first thing she must do is decide how many friends she and Ruffer will invite. Using addition helps her solve that problem; she uses addition to quickly figure out how many people will be invited without having to count them one by one. When they go to a supermarket to buy eggs, Nora and Ruffer use subtraction to find out which items are cheaper than others.

By connecting the concept of money to calculation, children can learn to extend their adding and subtracting skills to large numbers. Start teaching addition and subtraction of money with addition questions, for example: "How much will you need if you want to buy two ice creams that cost five dollars each?" Children will eventually learn to solve harder subtraction problems, for example: "How much would you have to pay if you got a one-dollar discount on a carton of ice cream that costs five dollars?" Having children figure out prices for small items at a store or calculate the scores of sports games are fun activities that will reinforce math exercises of adding and subtracting larger numbers.

One, Two, Three!
Adding and Subtracting

| **Activity Goal** | To learn to add and subtract new numbers
| **Materials** | 15 marbles
| **Players** | 3

1 Divide the 15 marbles evenly into three groups of 5 marbles. Decide which player will be the "calculator" for the first round. The player who sits to the left of the calculator for the first round will be the calculator for the following round, and this will be the pattern throughout the game.

2 Players sit in a small triangle facing the center. For every round, each player decides what quantity of marbles he/she will play with, from 0 up to 5 marbles. Each player then grasps that number of marbles in one hand (or picks up no marbles), without showing the others how many he/she is holding.

3 Players call out "Ready!" together, and all hold out their closed fists (with marbles concealed) to the center of the triangle they form. They then count "One, two, three!" while flipping their fists over and opening them to reveal the number of marbles each is holding.

4 The designated calculator adds up the sum of the marbles in the three players' hands. He/she details the addition process by saying, "Three plus two plus one equals six," for example. If the answer is right, all three players raise their arms in the air and say, "Hooray!"

5 The calculator for any given round can decide in advance to change the operation from addition to subtraction. If he/she plans to do so, he/she can hold only 1 or 2 marbles (or none at all, for 0). When it's time to play, he/she calls out "Minus!" As with the addition example, the calculator details the subtraction process for the calculation. He/she might say, "Four minus two minus one equals one," for example.

Addition and Subtraction Game with Ruffer

Ruffer is organizing all the items he used for his birthday party. He tells Nora to ask him an addition problem.

How many snacks are here in total?

5 lollipops +
3 cookies =
8 snacks +
2 chocolates =
10 snacks.

5
3
+ 2
—
10

6 plates + 3 straws
= 9 items + 1 balloon
= 10 items + 2 party poppers
= 12 items + 2 birthday cards.
When we add those
together we get 14 items.

How many items did we use for the birthday party?

6
3
1
2
+ 2
—
14